Swell

....

First published in 2015
by Rod Miller Publishing

All rights reserved
Copyright © Rivenrod 2015

The right of Rivenrod to be identified as author of this work
has been asserted in accordance with Section 77 of the
Copyright, Designs and Patents Act 1988

This book is sold subject to the condition that it shall not,
by way of trade or otherwise, be lent, resold, hired out
or otherwise circulated without the publishers prior consent
in any form of binding or cover other than that in which
it is published and without a similar condition including
this condition being imposed on the subsequent purchaser.

A CIP catalogue record for this book is available from the British Library.
ISBN: 978-1515307129

This book, Swell, is a work of fiction. Names, characters, places and
incidents are either the product of the author's imagination or, if even
remotely recognisable, used fictitiously. Any resemblance to actual persons
(living or dead), events, or locales is entirely coincidental.

Cover drawing: Rivenrod
Cover design: Norag Archipelago
Editorial/Proofreading: Sam Nash

Printed and bound by Createspace

Swell

....

by the same author:

Miscreation
Oh My God!

*(Coming soon, look out for these titles
at all your favourite retailers)*

Swell

by Rivenrod

*He could have run into the soft arms of Death,
instead he burrowed into sticky red earth
and lay very still, hardly breathing.*

Swell

···

a labour of love for
Annette,
Alexandria and Joshua,
Robert, Kristopher and Nicholas

Index

Part One (page 1)
A car pulls up and the sudden rhythmic throb of its engine catapults him to the ticket-window where, blinking wildly, he passes a ticket into the palm of an impatient disembodied hand.

Part Two (page 21)
"Successful hiding," she intoned in their private voice, "often relies on the compliance of *Outsiders*, even though most of them don't know they're doing it.

Part Three (page 57)
It was, however, the penultimate item in the morning's catalogue of aggravations that grieved him far more than any other, if for no other reason than it accentuated the malignant precariousness of human dependability.

Part Four (page 80)
She threw back her head and laughed at some unheard witticism and fiddled with the lobe of her ear followed by the clasp of a slim chain she wore around her glistening neck which bore a crucifix; Christ's feet nestled in the crease of her cleavage.

Definitions of Swell (swĕl)

v - Swelled or swol·len (swō′llən), swell·ing, swells

v.intr - To increase in size or volume as a result of internal pressure | To expand.

v.tr - To cause increase in volume, size, number, degree, or intensity | To fill with emotion.

n - A bulge or protuberance | A long wave on water that moves continuously without breaking.

In Music - A crescendo followed by a gradual diminuendo.

adj - Swell·er, swell·est

Informal - Socially prominent; stylish | Excellent; wonderful, good.

*"You must attend
to the commencement of this story,
for when we get to the end
we shall know more than we do now."*
Hans Christian Andersen

Part One

It is eight in the morning and even before starting work he knows the chances are he will kill himself at some time during the day.

On arriving at the hut he closes and locks the door, shrugs off his thin waterproof jacket, tugs out the creases by pulling each sleeve tight and hangs it by the loop from a hook on the door. He shuffles to turn around while stooping to avoid a naked bulb dangling from the ceiling by a twisted wire and quickly glances behind to make sure he has not set it swinging. He draws a slow stertorous breath, taps the tight knot of his tie three times and then in quick succession: stretches to full height: brushes a fringe of thick black hair from his eyes: dives into a plastic carrier bag: lifts out a Thermos flask (its lid and stopper stained with brown dribbles, like dried blood): pours tea into his mug: places it in its customary spot and pauses, his head completely motionless, transfixed it seems by the pattern of rings and curlicues in the layer of thick grey dust covering the window ledge while his brain hums behind liquid pale blue eyes, bewildered perhaps by some omission in his routine or suddenly preoccupied by an ancient, fleeting, reminiscence. But then, with a jolt, as if awaking from an unplanned nap, he arches his long back and with deliberate ease reaches into the carrier bag once more and extracts a plastic lunch-box containing a crab paste sandwich which he balances with trembling fingers on the ledge beside his mug. So far, so good.

Ducking and turning in one smooth motion he carefully positions himself in front of a shabby deck-chair, plucks trouser fabric up into his groin for comfort and gradually descends whilst bending forward to look between his knees, making sure his sturdy suitcase is correctly placed beneath as a precaution for when the threadbare canvas eventually tears through. Inch by inch he settles deeper, and as he recedes into the gloomy corner he leans to the side, pulls back a miniature curtain from a peep-hole no bigger than an envelope, roughly sawn through the wooden wall of the hut, and cranes his neck to squint through it at the world outside.

He sees no vehicles or people and is only vaguely aware of the dismal thrum of traffic emanating from beyond the bedraggled thorny hedge which borders the road and is the limit of his view. Satisfied, he rearranges the curtain and falls back into his corner, closes his eyes and drums his fingertips on the smooth surface of a stack of sharply folded newspapers beside him; he finds one every evening by the bins near the gate flapping on the ground like a wounded bird. For a fleeting second an expression, resembling a frown, passes across his lips and brow.

In a minute or two, he will pick up a mirror with a pink plastic frame and pull at the skin of his face searching for whiskers missed whilst shaving in his poorly lit bathroom.

Ten years ago, it had taken them three days to build his hut.

That summer the Council conscripted Italian prisoners of war to cut down trees in a field behind the picture house. Policy allowed them to overlook their indigenous army of demobbed soldiers who wandered the streets desperately in need of work. He was a young man then and had stood in the road, clutching his half-empty suitcase, eyes streaming from the smoke of crackling fires burning ripped branches, some of which had tiny green leaves clinging to them, like children. Fire finished the job axes and bow saws started. Those big belted, bare-chested men, glistening fiercely, hacked and scraped the rolling landscape until it was smooth, then covered it with shiny black tarmac. They made a car-park and painted the hut green in remembrance of the wild grass that once grew there.

It was in the same field when, as a child, his mother had taken his hand, the only time he could remember, and tugged him along, urgently hurrying, giddily floating, only for him to slip from her grip, stumble and graze his pristine skin. He remembered her touch and how it had been worth the bloodshed.

It is now 8:21am.

    He sits in his deck-chair cradling a mug of tea and there he remains for a minute or two, eyes closed, acclimatising himself once again to his makeshift kingdom. He stretches his long legs and welcomes the dim crush of emerging light. A contented sigh slips through his teeth and he allows the tacky remains of a dreamless sleep to stitch the current day into a seamless extension of the day before where the interruption of evening and night-time were nothing more than a vacant interlude in the ebb and flow of his existence.

    His lips purse a kiss and he gently blows the skin of his tea, then takes several staccato sips whilst perusing his collections of prized flotsam piled neatly on the foot-polished planks of the undulating floor. Along the wall opposite stands a pyramid of battered tin boxes of all shapes and sizes, their faded labels printed with primitive images of sailing boats and smiling, bouncy girls wearing swim-suits and straw hats with ribbons. Beside them stands a pillar of hub caps leaning drunkenly to the side, some have curiously designed letters and symbols embossed into their shiny, pitted skins. He has hung the most interesting of them on the wall where rare needles of sunlight cause them to wink. In the corner farthest from his chair lies a tumble-down heap of nuts and bolts, a cascade of shrapnel, some nuts united with their bolts while others remain orphaned. Further back into the corner are a dozen delicately engraved perfume bottles, geometrically arranged, none of which is completely empty. And finally, in pride of place it seems, beside the door, hangs a girl's dress with a torn hem along with a pair of binoculars.

A car pulls up and the sudden rhythmic throb of its engine catapults him to the ticket-window where, blinking wildly, he passes a ticket into the palm of an impatient disembodied hand. He notices the finger nails are long and clean. He quickly fidgets the offered coins into a grubby tin before he waves the car through and lurches back into inky black safety where he remains hunched and watchful. Every so often at the remotest sound, real or imagined, he scowls at the window.

Soon he will play his little game. In the dragging hours before the noonday rush he will trap a fly and peer at it between his slightly parted palms, mesmerised by its berserk buzzing. He will wait patiently for it to fall silent and only grant the hapless insect its life by flinging it into the bright world from whence it came if someone should arrive at the ticket-window within the hour. It cannot be just anyone though, not a random person asking directions or enquiring after a lost item, no, that someone, whoever it might be, he did not care, must come to his hut specifically to buy a parking ticket. He has always been unambiguous on that point. If no-one should come his palms will press together with tedious slowness until finally, fingers like forceps, he will hold up its tiny crushed body for inspection, before dropping it into his brimming fly jar.

After the Italian prisoners had gone, an official at the Council, sporting a luxuriant black beard dusted with what looked like flakes of dried skin, handed him a key and in the voice of a clergyman bored with delivering the same old sermon, told him that everything he needed would be inside the hut. He itched to get away but was only allowed to leave once the official had snatched his hand and given it a limp, slightly damp, shake; then he ran all the way from the Town Hall to the car-park, his suitcase banging against his knees with every stride. Once inside the gleaming green hut, in the dusty darkness, he found it was exactly as the official had said. Everything he needed for his job comprised only two objects, a folded deck-chair propped against the wall and a shiny metal money-box which someone had placed on the windowsill, its lid open.

He stood still, taking stock, then roused himself and set about choosing a place for his chair, an exercise he conducted with exacting attention to every perceived threat. He paced back and forth, his arms folded, peering at the window. He stood in each corner in turn, bending forwards and backwards then leaning from the hips, first to one side, then the other. He darted outside and using only his feet, measured the depth and width of each wall, stopping now and then to flip his hand like a pianist whilst grimacing, calculating perhaps whether approximate measurements would suffice, if only temporarily.

He had no friends or acquaintances and consequently knew no one to help him test his calculations or the position of his chair. He could not, however, tolerate miscalculation or oversight, so he ventured into town to the hardware store, where he purchased a bundle of sticks and a ball of string from which he created a web of sight lines.

He squatted down and from every angle squinted up at the ticket-window, fretting and fussing, gauging his exposure to anyone who might approach the hut from any direction. He measured and plotted every possible position then checked and rechecked, paced and evaluated, his arms outstretched and neck craning, to be sure he would be out of sight until the very last moment. It was imperative that, even on the brightest of summer's days, sunlight would never penetrate his hiding place and in winter he was to be cocooned in a paraffin-heated womb. So it was, every day afterwards, he looked out on a bright world framed in black like a television flashing and stuttering in a darkened room.

Later that first day he added an extra precaution; at eye level beside his chair, he cut a small hole in the wooden wall and dressed it with a miniature curtain. A secret peep-hole which gave him an unobstructed view of the entire car-park.

When he was a boy, his mother too had hidden him

from evil. She had the gift to recognise the devil's hand in places others did not dare to look. Whenever evil came calling she would hold him lightly by the collar and lead him to the cupboard under the stairs where he sat for hours on end, curled up on a suitcase, hugging a coat to his stiffening knees while deathly silence hummed at the base of his skull. He grew to know darkness, the changes in its texture and its shifting shapes in the inky swirl. Sometimes, he would peek through cracks in the door and look out on the sunlit passageway, but never once did he see anyone, good or evil. Most times he would doze until hushed voices nudged him and tugged drowsiness from him. Always there was the dead, dull ruffling of a heavy coat and the tap and scuffle of leather soles as his mother bustled evil out the front door. Seconds later, without a word, a key would turn in the lock and the little cupboard door would swing open an inch or two. He always waited for nightfall, hardly breathing, before daring to crawl outside.

  His mother paid penance so they might be redeemed.

It is now 12:00 noon and savage heat mocks him for his crisp shirt, his tie and sharply pressed trousers.

He sits patiently awaiting the usual onslaught of lunchtime browsers bound for the brand new shopping centre and presently car after car materialises out of blistering haze building to a queue, jostling and fretting like unruly schoolchildren. From interior dark, each car window produces a flapping arm that carelessly throws small change onto the counter in exchange for a pink parking ticket.

They are all different, these arms, and in his seclusion he likes to think they have been sent to him as specimens of the various types of people in the world. Some are muscular and gravy brown - ruthlessly assured: some are thin and china cup white - timid, anxious: some are thick and flabby, smelling of soap - indolent, blasphemous. He knows the provenance of every one of them in the same way he knows the make and model of a vehicle from the throb of its engine. He likes soft, doll-like arms best of all and fears those that hesitate, picturing their fingers curling around his wrist feeling for a pulse, drawing certain conclusions. Divining the character of a person from the type of arm they posses is a gift he has neither the opportunity nor inclination to share.

It is now 2:49pm and his head is reeling. The relentless swelter has turned the contents of his skull to liquid which sloshes in a lazy tide while reflected images thrown up into his eyes grow into bloated, ghostly faces swimming in ink within the cars. Coins become jelly to the touch and slip from his grip.

The last of the queuing cars have dispersed, slotting sheepishly into their allotted spaces as if scolded for their behaviour. With one last nodding sweep of the car-park he lurches backwards, reaching for his chair with the clumsiness of a man carrying a dead weight, groping his way around the walls, grasping any surface for support, twisting in his fist a sodden handkerchief which smells of fermenting cabbage and which fails to wipe away the needles pricking his eyes. Presently he will hear once again the smack of bullets slapping flesh.

―

He came of age at a time of war.

She wore a blazing smile, a blood-red gash against chiselled white teeth, and yet mother and son had not touched, or kissed as they bade farewell, but waved politely. He never looked back as he marched away awkwardly wooden in his stiffly pressed uniform and his suitcase, stuffed to bursting, gripped tightly at his side.

He thought of her constantly during endless nights swaying sleepless in the belly of the steaming ship, his skin slippery with sweat. At times he imagined her close by and watchful, stroking his hair and cheek, whispering into his ear while he pretended to sleep. And often in the twilight of his dreams he saw her cleaning and shifting in the parlour at home, bewitched by the soft sway of her body as she spread herself across the table, rhythmically scrubbing at a speck, her eyes expectant, her mouth half-smiling when she caught him watching her. Other times, it was her legs that mesmerised him; plump and firm, they swished busily beneath her floral cotton dress the hem of which wafted her faint scent of rose water and burnt toast. Then, as dawn broke, she would caution him to think only of her and deny the devil his temptations.

. . . be a good little soldier for your mummy

One morning the ship stopped heaving and shoulder to shoulder the soldiers marched their upholstered chests and jutting chins into a forest green furnace.

> GOLLY GEE IT'S REALLY SWELL
> TO SEND THOSE YELLA' MEN TO HELL! . . .

It was there those good ol' boys sallied forth two by two, expecting weaker prey, and caroused in a very un-private hell where bullet swarms hung in air made thin by a thousand breaths shocked to extinction. It was there they learned that in the clumsy, slow motion art of dying only the living scream.

In blazing dread, Death dissected bloody organs and flung them still pulsing at the stripped branches of trees - hung them like gaudy baubles at a bizarre banquet - while a raucous choir thundered a crashing overture to oblivion. Limbs, carelessly severed, crawled.

He could have run into the soft arms of Death, instead he burrowed into sticky red earth and lay very still, hardly breathing, peeking through a crack between splintered tree trunks until the roaring stopped and silence crept into his bones with the morning chill.

It is 4:16pm and the heat has reached suffocating maturity. He lies sprawled in his chair gulping air while all around him his precious things drown in boiling oil. Leaden fingers fumble aside the tiny curtain of his peephole and he gasps, his tongue a hot knife, his one spying eye seared by sudden brightness as muscles across his temples tighten and tear loose from the bone.

Outside the hut, bloated cars bask in a sluggishly slopping sea and crackling air shimmies along roasted metal while dazzling light bends and gyrates to primitive rhythms. From dips and hollows in the tarmac eddies of heat wrestle and writhe, skim to escape the scalding surface sideways only to quickly condense into breathless, exhausted ooze and die away. Meanwhile in his skull, a relentless beat drums harder and faster, incessantly louder and heavier and enters his body through his gaping, foaming mouth and dripping skin. Sound, tendons, gristle, the throbbing bass, bile, blood and bones beating, beating into him, becoming him. Booming in him, a reverberating core-less husk, shells exploding, skin stretched and burnt. Pounded, him pounding compounds of oxygen, hydrogen, nitrogen, a white-hot anvil. Beating, beating, beating.

Through mist and into his sagging eye steps a figure, a mirage, ragged at the edges, emerging limb by limb from wrinkles in the oven-baked battlefield. Gradually the smudge becomes a girl, a young woman, striding purposefully towards his hut and with each step a plume of dust jumps from the black tarmac as if she's under enemy fire. Closer, he notices a half-smile playing at the corners of her mouth; he licks his cracking lips and blinks salty sweat from his red veined eyeballs. He is transfixed by her short cotton dress clinging wetly to her legs, catching between them, defining her tight contours. His mouth falls slackly agape. He blinks and slowly becomes aware he recognises her. He could hardly dare to hope, but there she is, he sees her quite clearly now, it is the girl from the hardware store and she has come to save him. He blinks once more and reminds himself that she could not possibly know, how could she? But she's here anyway. Should he run to her?

... Mummy wouldn't like that

... instead he peeks out, and with a sniper's eye scrutinises every inch of her: breasts swinging and bouncing: the crook of her elbow: the curve of her hip:

firm thighs and the promise of a plump crotch. She, the object of thrilling untouched desire, blatantly unknowing her sexuality would stir him as nothing has ever done. How could she know?

> *... of course she knows, she's got the devil in her*

His stomach juices churn, his finger joints blister and begin to throb deep in the bone. His gaze returns to her face, her open vaguely smiling face, and he yearns to touch, to know with all his senses her virginal, pink flesh: to sift her golden hair between his fingertips: to lift the silken threads and create lace-work patterns against the sky: to cradle her cheek: to trace the slope of her shoulder round her body to the spine. He imagines her skin will be soft, slightly damp, trembling ...

> *... and right up close you can look down her top*

"Not now Mummy, please!" Molten lava rushes to his heart. He is unprepared but he knows the girl is coming for him and when she arrives he will catch her slender

hand, take her by the waist and fold her body into his
and . . . and . . .

> . . . *suck her wet tongue*

. . . nibble her rose bud lip and brush her coral ear softly, smoothly charm her with his hot breath.

> . . . *no boy, not like that! Suck the bitch dry. She hungers for you too, but you already know that don't you!*

"Tell me Mother, what does she want me for? Go on, tell me what she wants! What? . . ."

> . . . *to stuff her mouth with your greasy manhood, that's what. The slut!*

Now he leans forward, closer to the little window, preparing himself, but a shell explodes at close quarters and a thousand stinging shards slam into his chest. Such pain as never before existed slithers up his neck and hammers at his skull, "Oh god. Oh Mum . . ."

> . . . *so, you admit it, you do need me*

"Shut up Mummy!" and the peep-hole's miniature curtain scalds his palm as it rips from the wall.

. . . I'm all you'll ever need

"Mummy. Please. Please let me go!" He smells lavender and a desperate yell writhes like a snake in his throat but he is paralysed. Swimming in sweat, he watches bewitched as she guides his hand to the hem of her cotton dress - blood red poppies and forget-me-nots - and like so often before she helps his magic fingers make gooseybumps but his touch recoils from the cold, cold flesh of her belly and his broken voice produces nothing but a beseeching rattle, "she came for *me* Mummy. . . she came for me".

. . . yes son, Mummy knows.

The young woman from the hardware store now stands at the ticket-window of his hut. She smooths her dress, flexes her legs backwards and forwards, checks her reflection in the glass and tips her head slightly to the left - she thinks her right side is her best side - pleased with what she sees and still smiling she pauses for a single beat of her singing heart and then with a porcelain-white knuckle taps five times on the glass.

At that precise moment it is as if a bullet has pierced his electrified skin and burrowed to the centre of his heart, killing him.

Part Two

So, what's going on here? Is it reasonable to assume, do you think, there's more to this story than meets the eye?

Perhaps we should add a little more flesh to the bones then we might see whether we are right to believe what we think we know.

From the very beginning we are made aware that this man, our Car-park Attendant, binds himself to routines. No sooner has he arrived at the hut than he begins ticking items off a mental check list and, given his obvious self-absorption, it's a safe bet he would never allow himself any distraction whilst doing so. This small piece of information concerning his character might lead us to the impression he is a man who meticulously plots and plans a task before even embarking upon the first stage and only when it has been completed to his total satisfaction will he then proceed to stage two. Thus he will plod myopically through the task to its culmination regardless of the physical traumas he must endure to do so, even if it happens to be one of the hottest days on record, not with any sense of enjoyment but feeling instead a duty has been done. He is a stickler for detail too, to the point of obsession.

And what of his treasure, his prized flotsam, objects he has rescued by chance, old things people have thrown away or misplaced? His hut is crammed full of them - nuts and bolts, hubcaps and tin boxes - what is it about this stuff he finds so appealing? It is highly unlikely any of these items is a memento of a special occasion because there are far too many of them. A clue to his true intentions might lie in us knowing he went to a lot of trouble in choosing those specific items, then again there is nothing to prevent us thinking the perfume bottles or the hubcaps could just as easily be replaced by, say, bird's eggs or bubblegum wrappers. The most probable explanation for the collections of treasure is that he actually needs things - any type of thing - in order to assign stories and reminiscences, real or imagined, to them and those particular things just happened to be at hand. Of course, if that were the case, he could change what they mean to him at any time, if he wanted.

One thing is certain however, he treasures one particular item above all others and as such it's significance most likely remains constant. We are able to draw this conclusion purely from the pride of place it occupies; his sister's pretty little party dress hangs from a nail beside the door, directly opposite his deck-chair, always in plain view from every part of the hut. As it happens, for more years than he can remember he has carried it with him in his suitcase, tied in a neat bundle with a length of red wool. The dress and binoculars were the first and only personal things he brought from home to the hut when he began working there. But how did it come to occupy such a privileged position in his domain?

He was seven years old when, during one of their boisterous games, the hem of the dress caught on the buckle of his sandal and ripped. His sister had sucked her teeth in horror but her laughing eyes betrayed her. It was not that she felt no shame, it was just that to her, in a broader context, the dress was of no great significance. Daddy knew it too and told them not to worry, he would square it with Mummy. Daddy always did.

His sister stopped breathing soon afterwards. He was awoken early in the morning by a commotion outside his bedroom door, on the landing. Above the sound of his mother's whining distress and his father's anxious mumbling came the calming, level tones of a stranger's voice strident with heroic authority. He crept from his bed and inched the door open and saw the figure of a tall angular man in a green suit standing in the doorway of his sister's room. The man stooped his large pointed head whilst speaking to his parents. At that moment they appeared to be much smaller than they had been the previous day.

After dressing him, Mother retired to her room where she remained leaving the boy to sit alone on the edge of his bed, swinging his legs to and fro, watching his polished shoes flash from bright to dull in the sunlight and shadow, listening hard all the while for the rustle of footsteps. After the doctor had departed, it was Daddy who came and hovered in the doorway of his room unwilling or unable to speak, hanging his head.

In the space of a few days his father's big face had become shrunken, immobile and hard, and his eyes which had always been glittering windows to a bottomless pool of mischief and joy, were all smashed. The boy wondered if his tears which came often and rolled in wide wet streaks down his ashen cheeks had bits of glass floating in them. He had gripped his son's skinny shoulders as he guided him into his sister's room and, glancing at the body of his daughter lying tucked up in bed, said in a soft monotone, his tongue too large for his mouth and his miserable lips dripping, that he was sure his princess had gone to a better place and that she would not have wanted her little brother to be sad for very long because she was happy in her new home and had everything she needed. Anyway, one day they would all be together again and until then she wanted him to have something to remember her by, something special that belonged just to her.

It had not crossed the boy's mind he would ever need anything to help him remember his sister but his father coaxed him, willed him not to be scared and tried so hard to smile, to encourage the boy, but something prevented the corners of his mouth turning upwards.

The boy found himself pottering around her bedroom, picking at her dainty things, only to return every one of them to its exact same place. He foraged in cupboards for a favourite toy just as they had done a thousand times before at the start of one of their games, he half expected her to leap from the bed and whack him with a pillow but when he turned to look at her she was so still, so quiet it unnerved him.

The dress lay on her bedside chair, unfolded, as it would have been had she just taken it off to go to bed. He did not know how or why he came to pick it up, but somehow it found its way into his hand, neither could he think of any reason he felt compelled to ask his dead sister if he may have it as a keepsake, but he crept to her bedside anyway, held it to her cheek and gently stroked her skin with the soft cotton. The weight of silence grew unbearable.

For his next birthday, Daddy gave him his old binoculars saying they were from Mother as well, but when he thanked her and tried to kiss her, she turned her face and told him not to be silly, so he ran to Daddy and gave him an extra big hug for them both. It was only when they released each other he saw that although his father was smiling and looking in the direction of his mother, his eyes were focussed on a place a long way beyond her.

Four days later, he came in from the garden where he had been sent to play, and his mother told him his father had gone away, she was very sorry but she could not have him live with them any more. She sat in her parlour at the far end of the smooth sofa, straight-backed with several plump cushions in line at her back and her hands folded on her lap, her thin white fingers knotted together. She rocked continuously backwards and forwards, a sliver of dry pink tongue flicking between her taut lips, muttering. He asked her why Daddy had gone: where has he gone? Will he come home when he's hungry? What if he gets cold? Mummy had always worried people would catch their death of cold; she did not answer but stared through him at the netted window, every now and then she pressed the back of her hand to the end of her nose and sniffed.

He sat perched on an armchair opposite her for a very long time, his feet dangling, attempting to nail down all the events of the days and weeks just gone, trying to work out what had happened, expecting her to say something, to explain, but his mother remained motionless, tight-lipped and hard eyed, and everything in that cold room gravitated to her, was sucked into her in the same way living light is absorbed and quenched by a stellar black hole until all around him nothing remained except steely darkness and the beating of the clock in the hall which ticked louder and louder, filling his head and squeezing water from the corners of his eyes and down his nose.

Suddenly his meditation was severed by a lightening bolt. Reality was brutally reattached to his torpor by his mother springing to her feet and shouting from the hallway for him to follow, she banged open the front door and set off briskly, almost running, down the street. He kept up as best he could and in no time they reached the field behind the picture house where he had to stop and catch his breath. His mother came back for him, took his hand and dragged him along so breathlessly fast he tripped on the uneven earth, fell and grazed his knees. She hoisted him from the grey dirt and brushed him down with her handkerchief wondering aloud what she had done to deserve such a clumsy boy while she fingered his hair back in to place. She almost, but not quite, hugged him and if only for that tentative brush of motherly connection, he was glad his knees throbbed and were bloody. By the time they reached the bus station, unsurprisingly the bus had already departed with his father on board.

Since that day, until he went to war, he kept a suitcase packed in the cupboard under the stairs just in case.

It should be noted he did not shed a tear, not even after having suffered a painful fall which resulted in his knee being deeply cut by a sharp flint buried in the grass.

For weeks and months afterwards, he spent every waking hour missing his father. It was a time of bleak bewilderment. The house echoed emptily while every ledge and shelf were consumed by deepening layers of dust. The air indoors was moist and stale, laced with mildew, which clung to fabrics and furniture and perspired with the odour of wet laundry left too long in the basket. Night followed day and day followed turbulent sleep which always began with dreams of sunshine and joy, singing and the bright shiny faces of his father and sister, only to end long before dawn in crushing despair as she and Father were whisked whimpering from his embrace by growling wingéd shapes. In the suffocating chaos he always found himself standing helplessly aside, uncontrollably giggling, hating himself.

It was during this time his mother started teaching him how to hide. She began by explaining that hiding was not a contingency but an art and a discipline, requiring rigorous planning, diligent application of the rules, which she would teach him, and meticulous execution. (Although she preferred to describe it as hiding, the art was more akin to making himself invisible even when in plain view.) She coyly suggested there might be extra rewards for applying himself and becoming good at it although she would not say exactly what those rewards might be. After a few days he realised the treacly whisper in which she lectured him was also a part of the exercise and he began to mimic her. Their ears quickly attuned to the other's husky intonations which, over the following weeks, developed into their own private means of communication, indecipherable by *Outsiders*.

After a few more months had passed certain elements of their structured existence metamorphosed into games and wagers. Together they invented a means of testing random chance against certainty, for example a predictable event unexpectedly not happening would in turn trigger something certain that would definitely happen. A cold bath would be the inevitable consequence of a bus unpredictably not arriving on time at the stop across the road. A neighbour's kitten which strayed into their house one winter's evening initiated a game where, if no one knocked to enquire after its whereabouts by the end of the following day, the kitten would be drowned.

Time passed and their games became ever more complex with increasingly painful consequences. However, they themselves deemed their pleasures to be simple.

Every evening they hunched over the kitchen table, he standing on a chair, darkness held at bay by a single bulb burning above them, their two heads pressed together, muttering and whispering as if the sombre corners of the room concealed spies. Step by cautious step the mistress and her young protégé developed their games and routines, keystones of the art, rendering the unfamiliar familiar, plotting the elements of their daily lives not so much in terms of what needed to be done but rather by the extent to which their alliance might be compromised. Over time, their routines evolved into impenetrable structures raised up against the world and all its dangerous realities. Routines became the backbones, the spinal threads of their existence where every interlocked task was performed automatically, without thought, becoming such an integral part of their consciousness everyday processes were stripped to the bone revealing a sequence of essential functions performed only in such ways as to preserve their invisibility.

Almost a year to the day after his father had gone away a difficulty arose which had potentially disastrous implications. Since a breadwinner no longer lived with them, there was no regular income with which to pay bills or provide food and other essentials to sustain them. The money she had saved for a family holiday, and the small amount her husband had left her, was all but gone and there was no clear way to resolve the practicalities of their physical survival. The obvious solution was for her to take a job, but that meant she would have to leave her son alone in the house while she ventured into the world outside. She would be thrust into unfamiliar environments and would have no choice but to interact with people, strangers. In such circumstances it was most likely the boy would be forced eventually to do likewise and their unseen life together, their alliance, would almost certainly not remain intact. Day after day, the boy watched his mother become more and more distracted and he too felt the weight of their predicament.

One morning, after a night of fitful sleep dreaming of improbable schemes, he ran into the garden and retrieved the toys he had buried there some months before, he washed them under the tap at the back door and lined them up on the window sill to dry. He was sure someone in the neighbourhood would buy them for their child to play with. He ran inside to tell his mother the plan and found her sitting on the edge of her chair, transfixed by the empty fire grate, deep in thought, lost in its dust and ashes. She was either unaware of his presence or wilfully ignored him.

The face she wore was one he had seen many times; whenever she calculated risk or unravelled mental knots: eyebrows raised: eyes wide increasing light energy to nourish her brain: cheeks, blotched pink in the flush of embarrassment: lips, mobile, continuously working. Her fingers fiddled with the curls at the nape of her neck then, as a dawning rose, she gingerly tinkered with the fragments of a smile tugging at the corners of her mouth.

Certain though he was she would scoff at the idea of selling his toys, recently buried and which he had thought never to lay eyes on again, he pressed on regardless and his noble words tumbled over themselves in the rush to escape. When he had finished she stared at him for several minutes then, with seemingly a great sacrifice of effort, she quietly told him he was far too soft for his own good and made him promise never to doubt her again. He mumbled into his hand and hung his head into which was suddenly thrust a terrifying vision of a boy very much like himself hanging by a slender twig high on a chalky rock face.

She ignored his sighs and said she had thought through their dilemma and had only just that minute come to realise the solution had been staring her in the face all along. She would work from home, in the guest bedroom, and she would begin the day after next because there were things to attend to beforehand. Her voice became terse and businesslike when she suddenly declared cleanliness to be akin to saintliness and she must remove all risk of infection and disease by thoroughly scrubbing and polishing her new work-room up side and down, including the tops of the doors and the carved parts of the skirting boards, and she must take up the carpet, hang it on the washing line and beat it soundly to remove the dust and mites that may be lurking in its scanty pile.

Breathing ever more heavily, she counted off on her fingers a list of things she must do before she could begin her new occupation until finally, swallowing a large gulp of air, she told him he must run to the florist in the morning to buy fresh spring flowers and a large bottle of witch hazel.

Her choice of occupation enabled them to survive in the world without being wholly a part of it. It serviced a primal need whilst also being an appeasement to the devil, and the money was good. Her clients were faceless, her encounters with them meaningless, there was no emotional currency or warmth in their coupling. From the outset, it was imperative for her to detach what she allowed those men to do to her from the bond she had constructed with her son. But she could never let her guard slip because if, by some accident, he was ever exposed to those men, however casually, he would be instantly paired with her, an association would be made between her son and the nature of her work, and that was unthinkable. Who knows where that might lead. Everything she did was driven by the necessity to keep him for herself, while he was still young and so impressionable it was vital he be kept separate from the Outside at all costs and to that end, minutes before being engaged in business, she would hide him in the cupboard under the stairs, not purely from a sense of embarrassment but also as a precaution against the unpredictable.

It should be noted that while she was preparing the guest room, touching up the paintwork on the walls, the sleeve of her work coat caught on the hook of the paint kettle which caused the brush laden with paint to fall to the floor. It was long after midnight before the stain was removed from the carpet to her satisfaction.

And so we arrive at an age in the life of our Car-park Attendant when he must navigate the tricky path from childhood into adolescence and school. At school, he was daunted at first by the timetables which governed every aspect of his activities however, he soon discovered with some relief he would have little trouble working them into his own routines. It is true that every minute of every school-day was allocated to a certain task or lesson but being a system or a construct of a routine, it was something he was familiar with. Of course he had to make some adjustments because school timetables are concerned with a number of fixed points ranged across the day relating to a series of set functions, each taking place at a specific location and at a specific time. His concerns therefore were with the spaces between those specific functions, black holes of potential chaos and danger, which had to be plugged. To be sure of finding robust solutions, leaving nothing to chance, he wrote out endless lists noting the minutiae of every day life at school: diagrams of routes to classrooms: teachers' whereabouts at given times of day: maps of corridors, when in use, by whom and when empty: the time at which teachers collected post from their pigeon-holes, and so on. He input the data into spidery matrices - blueprints for the avoidance of human contact - detailing every manoeuvre he must make, every route he must take.

Rarely, but too often for complacency, one or other of his peers, or a teacher, unexpectedly took a different route, or was late, and the matrix of his routines was utterly confounded. The formidable structure of his torturous procedures lay in ruins forcing him to scurry along on tiptoe, hugging the walls, his head to the floor, hardly breathing. It puzzled him he was never confronted. His mother explained there were probably a million reasons why he wasn't bothered by anyone but she was sure the main one was they did not actually want to see him. "Successful hiding," she intoned in their private voice, "often relies on the compliance of *Outsiders*, even though most of them don't know they're doing it. They don't notice anyone else, especially not a quiet boy like you who's good at hiding because they're too wrapped up in themselves". But, she warned him, people, particularly children, can be sneaky. When least expecting it, one or other of them might do something nice and pretend to be friendly, make absurd promises, lies of course, just to trap him but, she said, "the Devil is in every one of their blackened hearts so it's best to steer clear of them all!"

Luckily, she would always be close by to watch over him.

⁓

Puberty was a particularly distressing period not least because the wiring in his brain had suddenly became entangled. Nothing made sense any more and everything about his life was unfair. Breathing, walking, eating; every microscopic nuance connected with the act of living was boring and bound, somehow, to end in catastrophe. The territory through which he was being forced to travel was unfamiliar to him.

When left to his own devices he would sleep long into the afternoon festooned by the clothes he had worn the day before, barely half removed. His bed had become a swamp upon which he drifted in open mouthed stupefaction and yet when he did manage to drag himself from his foul smelling pit the energy coursing through his body was boundless. He was physically incapable of remaining still. One minute he twirled like a ballerina, the next he would throw himself at the floor where he would lie panting, running a nail along the cracks between floor boards, then suddenly stand, then sit, then stand, then sit again crossing and uncrossing his legs. He felt freakish, dirty and permanently hungry, and all the while a chaos of seething worms spread through him like a virus, just beneath the skin, itches he could not scratch.

More terrifyingly, the routines he had so meticulously constructed were suddenly alien to him, the lists he had relied on for so long seemed to have been scrambled, the more he studied them the more stubbornly confusing the words and matrices became. He stared and stared and the neat rows of numbers and notations ravelled and unravelled, eventually congealing into quarrelsome bundles of wire and springs. Even his school textbooks seemed to be crammed with indecipherable gobbledegook, invariably he found himself losing interest mid-way through a passage and had to read the same lines over and over, he even traced the letters with his finger to prevent them detaching and drifting into thin air. He had to stab them repeatedly to keep them in place until his nail ripped and made a bloody trail across the page. Daytime was a blur of contradictions, and at night he dreamed of a skirt's warm hem swaying, revealing then concealing, or a work coat with buttons missing. All too often, he awoke to a sticky wetness on his thighs, his brain a cauldron of burning shame, and a dawning recognition that his life might never be as reliably uncomplicated as it had been.

Without the subject ever being discussed, it was as if his mother knew already the nature of the changes taking shape within him and yet she added spark to the flame of antagonism between them by allowing aspects of their relationship to be characterised by stark contrasts: he wanted one thing from her and she would give him the equal and exact opposite: he raged, she whispered: he demonstrated his independence, she crowded him with cosseting advice: he craved space, needing to have some distance between them, she kept him close and watched him like a hawk. Occasionally she made demands of him and whereas in his earlier life he would have jumped to and obeyed her to the letter he now froze in a state of sullen shock, suddenly arousing himself to berate her for disturbing his peace - "Can't you see I'm busy!" - even when he was not. At times he felt he was a creature mounted in a bell jar, an object, coveted as precious only in death, ogled and criticised only by his mother. And there was nothing more irritating than her uncanny ability to read his state of mind or the fact she was right. She was always right! It was her smug face and contrariness he so despised.

Increasingly, over the previous two or three years, it had become difficult for him to remember a time when it had been anything other than him and his mother against the Outside, but now the stockade of their common reclusion was in danger of being breached, not by anyone or anything from the Outside, but by themselves from the inside, by their own discongruity.

Then, one winters' day the construction of their relationship was abruptly and conclusively transformed. As usual he had remained in the house all day having no desire whatsoever to venture outside, other than into the enclosed garden. It was his habit to occupy his time with reading, preparing his school work for the coming day or the week ahead or sitting at the corner table in the large and airy kitchen reviewing his routines and matrices. On this particular day however, he simply loafed around oozing an inconsolable bad humour which clogged the atmosphere, managing to irritate both his mother and himself.

He lounged at the kitchen table picking holes in its plastic cloth, swinging his legs to an imagined beat and scuffing the soles of his shoes on the linoleum floor while his mother busied herself preparing their evening meal. Not a word passed between them even though his agitation, his incessant tapping and scraping, caused her to raise her eyes to the ceiling and force hot breath down her nose.

She replaced the scrubbing brush on the draining board and unhurriedly opened a side drawer, picked out a small paring knife from amongst the neatly arranged utensils and began to peel a potato. With each long cut, a curl of freckled skin dropped onto the pages of a newspaper she had spread on the draining board and with every third or fourth curl, she dipped the knife into the sink, half filled with browning water, and swished it vigorously backwards and forwards, punishing the water or the knife for the rising foulness of her temper. She kept her back turned against the boy who slouched scowling behind her and so they remained, the minutes ticking by, until her furious scraping dwindled in exact time with a relapse in the boy's histrionic tut-tutting, and silence reigned. A silence cut a few seconds later by the legs of the chair on which the boy was sitting suddenly slamming into the floor. His mother, having put down the knife, pressed both hands into the worktop and hung her head to her chest, breathing deeply. She may have considered the explosive racket was an expression of his hostility towards her or a signal he was almost ready for the lesson she had been planning to teach him for the last few days. She decided to wait until the ripples of tension had abated before acting on one or other of those options and thrust her neck forward to scrutinise, through narrow eyes, the weather beyond the window and the patterns of frost forming in the corners of the glass panes. Upon reaching the tenth deep breathe, she turned slowly around to face him, leaned back, crossed her arms and rested her eyes on the top of his head.

The force of her will drilled into his skull, and he sensed it. No doubt he wished he could quietly rise and deliberately stare her full in the eye, and continue to do so without wavering until it was she who faltered and bowed her head to the floor. But he would not. He could not. He knew he would remain seated fiddling with his fingers while her steady gaze probed him from head to toe, taking note of every twitch, every pulse, however slight. He would soon learn she could penetrate with disarming ease the veneer with which he had only recently begun to encrust himself. He had thought he wanted, needed, a shell as much to contain the passions seething within as to hide them from her laser-like perception.

"Well, young man," she began in a small wheedling voice, emphasising the word man, charming him as a snake might charm a rat, "what's going on inside that head of yours?" He squinted at her from the side of his face, shrugged his thin shoulders and his mouth began to frame a challenge, what do you mean? but before his audible voice could catch and project the words she interrupted, "just tell me what it is, I need to know what's bothering you so I can help."

When cornered by a stronger predator a small animal in the wild will tend to retreat as far into shadows as it can and will rarely pluck up whatever courage it may have within it to make a counter attack. However, if on the very rare occasion it does make a stand and fight one would expect it to do so vigorously and with all the viciousness it can muster, after all it has nothing to lose. However, surprisingly, more often than not it will make only a half-hearted effort as if preserving its own life is hardly worth the trouble. No, the most common defence of the trapped animal is to curl up into a furry ball, crush itself as far as it can get into the shadows and pretend to sleep, presumably to suppress the dread of being torn to shreds. The ultimate denial.

The boy found himself trapped, and without shadows in which to hide decided against standing up for himself, instead he folded his body inwards, hunching over like a miserable wretch in imminent danger of punishment. Doubtless he felt naked and vulnerable.

"You must tell me what's worrying you because I'm your mummy," she said, "and that's what Mummy does isn't it. Mummy makes worries go away." He looked up at her and shrugged again though more uncertainly this time, "you mustn't cause Mummy any trouble must you because we both know what trouble means don't we?" Very slowly he began to nod.

"I can't hear you." she snapped.

"Yes," he muttered.

"It means *Outsiders* will come and take you away from me doesn't it." She must have noticed the panic in his eyes, so made her voice tremble, "then I'll have no-one, will I. I'll be all alone," still he remained silent, "and no one will care if I live or die."

With a sniff his mother reached behind her to the

draining board for a cloth and finding it, embarked upon a ritual of rubbing each finger in turn of her already dry hands.

"So tell me," she said her voice more firm, "tell me, just tell me". The boy stole a glimpse of her from beneath his beetling brow and shifted uneasily in his chair. His tongue was dry and stuck to the roof of his mouth but the images in his head were slick and wet and the skin of his legs felt hot and had started to itch.

"Just tell me!" she yelled.

The boy jumped and barked an anguished cry, "I don't know how to tell you! I don't know what's wrong with me . . ."

"Insolence and . . ." she hissed, "and wilful disobedience! You're a nasty, horrible son to your mother."

His lips parted but only to allow a rushing sigh to pass between them.

On the table next to him was a food storage bell, a wicker frame covered with lace netting, the boy fixed his attention upon it and after a while an image came to him of a spider trapped inside it. He could see it, at the rim, rubbing its front legs together in prayer, with a tear dropping from each of its eight eyes.

"Insolence and lies!" She threw the cloth at the table narrowly missing his head, "not telling me is the same as lying. Lying! Have I taught you nothing? Has everything I've done for you been a waste of time? Perhaps I should throw you out eh. Let the bully boys and murderers and thieves squabble over the choicest cuts of you. Outside, your hide isn't worth that!" She snapped her fingers. It sounded like a whip cracking.

He rubbed the back of his neck aggravating an angry soreness which was bedding into his skin. A hunger simmered in his stomach and loins. He needed to eat something sweet, anything. The relief would be as sudden and as luxuriously painful as peeing after having held water in his bladder for a very long time. He blinked, hating how he could be so easily distracted.

"Shall I tell you what's wrong with you? Eh! Because I already know what a lying, conniving, ungrateful little boy thinks about when his mother is slaving to keep a roof over his head and food in his belly." She paused, the effect was dramatic. "Filth and fancies, that's what. Your head is full of girls! Filth! Filth and girls! Am I wrong? Go on I dare you, tell me I'm wrong?"

And when his sullen silence rose to meet her, "I thought as much . . . you, you're no better than all the rest of them," she spat the words, "the boy who would be a man!"

He whispered, barely audibly, "I don't know what's wrong with me. Honestly I don't" He remained motionless, anticipating a barrage, his long thin legs stretched out in front of him, his hands in his pockets, he scowled at his shoes. Her perception of his distress and its causes was uncannily accurate but still he would not give her the satisfaction of acknowledging it. Stony faced she stared straight ahead, stared right through him. The clock in the hall clanged the hour at the very moment something inside her snapped and she slumped forward against the sink, her spirit seemed to slide from beneath her, she nodded two or three times in slow motion. A decision, long in the brewing, had been made. She rubbed her hands on the tea-towel again, heaved a sigh and muttered to no one in particular that for the sake of peace and to preserve his soul, like any good mother, she would have to take care of things herself. "Men indeed! The devil take them."

The boy was undoubtedly startled because his movements, subtle though they were, became jerky, disjointed and he peered around vacantly into all four corners of the room. When he eventually found her eyes, the hardness in them had melted and was close to spilling over. He was mesmerised by a globe of liquid dithering from the lash of her left eye, hanging by invisible thread, sagging to the very limit of its surface tension. He found himself wishing it would fall. What if she brushed it away? He caught his breath. No, she would never drop her guard. Suddenly the globe shuddered, contracted into a tight bead and vanished back to where it had come from. He breathed again and for a split second wondered if his father had gone away, for the sake of peace.

Had we been present the first time she went to him, we would have been hard pressed to understand what was going through her mind as she entered her son's darkened bedroom and quietly pushed the door to behind her, leaving a slight gap. She paused and a sliver of light projected onto her body, carving out the contours in a single strand, a thigh, a hip and her face whose skin was so white and flawless it could have been a mask. The movement of her limbs as she eased herself to his bedside were measured, choreographed, graceful and quiet, like that of a mourner at the death bed of a body well loved.

Although we might have some idea of what she's about to do, no expression, no sound she made or aspect of her demeanour betrayed any emotion whatsoever. In fact so calm and professional was she that nothing could lead us to doubt she was performing anything but a necessary duty.

She waited in silence beside his bed, her arms limp by her sides, her knees pressing the stark white counterpane, sensing the chill, and watching his eyelashes flash and flutter as he drifted into the twilight of sleep. It was only when his eyes ceased twitching and were finally still that she stirred and gently brushed the back of his hand with her fingers. When he was a child, a baby, she often slipped from her own bed where her husband quietly snored, and crept into the room her son and daughter shared just to watch him sleeping, marvelling at the perfection of his little mouth, his toes, his chubby pink fists and tiny nails, paper thin and translucent. To her mind, then, he was immaculate.

And now, encouraged perhaps by his dreamy acquiescence she quickly reached beneath the bed clothes and taking her fisted grip of him, with businesslike precision, she rapidly brought her obligation to a crowning conclusion.

It should be noted he was surprised at the softness of her hand, and his skin did not rip. Furthermore, his mother, bearing in mind her keen preoccupation with the practicalities of cleanliness, at some time during the night-time hours placed a pile of freshly pressed handkerchiefs on his bedside table.

And so to war and a time when he did in fact come of age.

Eighteen months after war began he was called upon to serve in the army. In distinct opposition to the complexities of puberty and attending school, he was completely at ease with the faceless regimen of army life, so much so that after only a few short weeks of training he confidently suspended his own routines in favour of the Sergeant Major's orders.

War: he overheard people, often civilians and sometimes soldiers a good distance from the front-line, arguing about war using words like love and hate, courage and bravery, pride and humility and marvelling at the notion that war must make a man feel really alive and how being there, being in the thick of it, in the firing line, where everything that happened was in the moment and where one of those moments could be the precise second they might know first hand exactly what it means to be a man and live to grow stronger by the experience. Or perhaps to die.

Extremes of passion are always involved in war but he felt none of them, instead he stood and observed. Every day, in every soldier's dreadful glance into the dense bush and in every gesture, even in the eyes of the enemy, he witnessed unrelenting terror. Surely not of death itself, because ultimately they knew that the actual point of dying is easy and painless, a blesséd relief. Their fear was of being subsumed by a living hell of agonies without end, of their minds becoming numb to living within humanity with bodies so ripped and mutilated Death would be wished for, prayed for, screamed for, begged for. Those soldiers were men picked from fields, factories and offices, some were boys not long out of the schoolroom, many of them had been shamed by their neighbours and friends into signing their youth away while others were summoned by anonymous letter just as our Car-park Attendant had been. Every man jack of them were herded together and despatched to remote places where they did dreadful things to other human beings without question even when every natural fibre in their bodies urged them to run from it as fast as they possibly could. Fear was the common truth that brought them together and imbued them with a desperate kind of camaraderie, bringing comfort for only a brief spell, lasting only so long as each of them drew breath. He, along with what remained of his troop, huddled in hastily dug pits in pitiless rain with their heads bobbing on their chests like feeding birds. He took no part in their senseless jabbering, their endless joking and bantering lies; he hardly spoke, but when on the rarest of occasions he was asked about his life back home he replied, without eye contact, "it's average". He earned the nickname, *Wraith*.

His war was brutal and short, sent to a jungle in Malaya attached to an American Division beefed up with gung-ho determination to smash the Japanese Imperial Army and drive it into the sea as recompense for the destruction of Pearl Harbour.

WHAT IN HELL WE WAITIN' FOR . . .

It soon became apparent the Japanese were not in such

awe of the American military machine as the Americans themselves were and had other ideas. Despite their marching chants -

> GOLLY GEE IT'S REALLY SWELL
> TO SEND THOSE YELLA' MEN TO HELL! . . .

- despite their training, their body armour and their flame-throwers, he was the only survivor when his platoon was ambushed and all around him young men and boys, the infinitesimal cogs in a megalithic machine, were flayed alive by ferocious gunfire.

When his section officers debriefed him they called the soldiers of his platoon, *poor devils* and *cannon fodder*. It was noted, however, that he seemed untouched both mentally and physically by the carnage he had lived through and so a week later he was posted to India and given the more sedate occupation of boxing ammunition.

Three years and four months after marching away a great silence fell upon the world, the fighting ceased and he returned home to be met at the bus station by a military clerk, brandishing a heavy metal clipboard, who demanded his name and address. Upon receiving his reply, the man stared at him, searching his eyes, then whipped a manilla envelope from beneath the sprung clip and handed it to him with a flourish. The letter, written in an efficient scrawl, informed him his mother had been found by chance, alone in her house, suffering from severe malnutrition and tuberculosis. She had been taken to a hospital where, he was assured, the doctors did all they could but alas to no avail, her life could not be sustained. She died nine months and five days after he was sent to war.

    And now alone in his hut he too has died.

Part Three

Some among us know only too well that a chain of events culminating in a catastrophe or a celebration can be set in motion days, weeks and sometimes years beforehand. It is often difficult to say exactly when or how a particular happening or set of circumstances came about which started the ball rolling, it is however an unassailable fact that in order for there to be an ending there must also have been something to trigger a beginning no matter how insignificant it may have seemed at the time.

    The prelude to our Car-park Attendant's particular tragedy began on the Wednesday evening just gone when he noticed the electric light bulb in the bathroom had begun to flicker which, experience had taught him, was a sure indication it was about to fail. To most of us a bulb on the blink is nothing more than a minor inconvenience, to him though it was a catastrophe, a devastating reminder his lists and routines, which he relied upon to rule every aspect of his household, were not foolproof. No matter how meticulously he noted the dates and times household items were due to be replaced, the location in which they were stored (in the case of light bulbs, in the cupboard under the sink) and when to purchase more, there could never be any guarantee the integrity of the information would remain intact. It could go wrong without a moment's notice rendering the whole exercise utterly futile. According to his records the light bulb in the bathroom had been replaced only ten days previously and, because his system did not allow for the unpredictable, it was with petulant alarm he noted there were, as yet, no spare bulbs in the cupboard. Outwardly, he remained determinedly un-flustered whereas inwardly his stomach knotted into a tight ball, his head began to pound and his blood seethed with rage at his own stupidity. He grabbed a pencil and holding it far too tight, as if doing so would ensure no further interference from the hand of fate or whatever people were calling it in those days, he scribbled a curt note to himself - Bulbs - and placed it on his sandwich box as a reminder to buy some on his way to work in the morning.

The next day, Thursday, he duly called at the hardware store and selected four light-bulbs each of which he held up to the light and squinted under the frosting to check the filaments were intact before handing them one by one to the proprietor who wrapped each in a ball of newspaper and gingerly nestled them in a brown paper bag which he swung around twice to twist the corners tight. Just as he was about to ask how much he owed, the proprietor suddenly barked and stamped his foot. Instantly a girl jumped up from beneath the counter and stood half crouching, gripping the collar of her starched white shop-coat. He towered over the girl, his piggy eyes like two shiny black buttons poked through the pendulous flesh of his huge red face. She stared around wildly, hunched like a rabbit run to ground, then ducked away, defending herself, when the proprietor suddenly clamped his hand to his mouth, extravagantly theatrical and not quite preventing himself bursting into fits of giggling.

The girl ignored her employer and blinking hard turned her gaze to the customer's face where it remained fixed, constrained from moving away by the obstinate glue of recollection, though in her mind the immediate impressions refused to be still, they persisted in being slight and fluid. She vaguely recognised the features, his handsome forehead and lock of black hair straying towards his dark brown eyes, the angular nose and tightly creased ears like flowers opening to accept the sun's warm rays, but she could not for the life of her place him. She blinked hard again, several times, imagining him in different contexts while a flash bulb in her brain attempted to match him with the images she tried desperately to fix to the walls of her memory. She smiled at him anyway because he seemed to be nice and she would be ashamed when she did remember where she had seen him and she had been unpleasant or rude.

For his part, he recognised her immediately, how could he not, his shoulders dropped a little as the subtle comfort of familiarity washed through him and he quickly regained his composure. His hands, however, continued to quaver and the palms remained damp. To relieve the itch he rubbed them as discretely as he could down his thighs.

He had first taken notice of her some two months earlier but only in the way a person might sense rather than truly see an object has been added to a familiar landscape. Over the following two weeks, day by day, she gradually seeped into his consciousness until, like pavements and kerb stones, she also became a staple component of his routine walk to work. After a few more days, he caught himself deliberately seeking her out and the thought and vision of her grew within him. He transfixed her to his mind, knitting images and dreamy impressions of her into his desires and yet, no words had ever passed between them. Whenever there was a close encounter and one of them became aware of the other they would not exchange glances or smiles but turn their eyes to the pavement or their separate shadows and discretely nod their heads. For want of knowing her real name he called her *Poppy*, which seemed to match her wispy blonde hair, pale green eyes and full red lips.

His eyes chased the bag of light bulbs from the proprietor's hand to the counter as his fingers leafed through his wallet and extracted a pound note. Poppy swayed towards him and whipped the money from his hand with a curious pincer-like stabbing motion and all the while her eyes did not leave his face but feasted on it. He leaned away to properly focus on her and found her lips were slightly parted revealing rows of even white teeth and a thin pink tongue. At her neck his slippery gaze absorbed the tantalising fact that the top two buttons of her shop-coat were missing leaving behind two pathetic tails of dark thread which, he thought, resembled tiny worms burrowing into her chest. A third button had come undone and had been left as it was, beneath it in musky shadow he could just see the bodice of a cotton dress printed with small blue flowers.

He returned to her face and saw she was smiling broadly, not just with her lips and cheeks, but the whole of her face and an ember glow emanated from within her. She finally recognised him. Their eyes locked together though in each there sank a separate dread into the pit of their innards, each beheld a fear of some mortal sin committed that would force them to part. The air around them grew thin. Sounds - the rattle and hum of everyday existence from within their bubble were muffled, confessional; and the light, the same morning light that had flooded his eyes when first he gazed upon her, was sucked outwards and away from them, out through the dazzling plate glass window and through the door to settle like a shimmering blanket on the pavement outside. Inside, shadows were bulked by cowering uncertainty, a dense blackness crushed into the corners and dusty crevices of the shop-floor.

The proprietor's greedy face turned to the girl whose own face now gave up it's blameless charm to her customer. They were frozen in time, the three of them, bound by a momentary bond which rooted them to the spot as time trickled past into an unplumbed maw of silence. His head swam, his eyes pricked, his mouth was dry and he found he had ceased to breathe; his swollen lungs throbbed, nagging at him from within his chest, burning the walls of his rib-cage, until finally instinct compelled him to draw breath.

Little by little, emerging from fog, came the proprietor's bloated shape and gloating smile. The Car-Park Attendant blinked several times, deliberately flexing and furrowing the muscles of his brow, and there he was, clearly now, the proprietor laughing extravagantly at him, winking at him over Poppy's shoulder and almost instantly he retreated into the familiar dullness of fear and humiliation; the spell was broken. He dropped his head as her slender white fingers pressed small change into the still damp palm of his trembling hand.

Such naked connection with anyone, let alone a

stranger of the opposite sex, had never happened before and in his confusion and excitement he had walked from the store without his light bulbs.

───

Though significant, the light bulb incident was not the only noteworthy milestone on the road to his eventual demise. No, the next event, or to put it more accurately - non-event - was an indication that the universe he had trained himself to inhabit so inconspicuously was out of kilter, setting him upon a dangerous orbit. Whether he could read the signs and understand their significance or not is a different matter and a question to which we may never know the answer. Nevertheless, let us continue exposing the bald facts of the tale.

On the evening of the same day his routine had been irredeemably ruined when he was unable to complete one crucial part of it. There was no newspaper.

Every evening since his first day at work, he had found a newspaper lying discarded in or around the rubbish bin at the gates to the car-park. And every evening he would retrieve it, take it home, iron it flat and carry it into work the following morning. He would not read it, he had read none of them because News was of no interest to him, but he would place it, pressed pristinely smooth, on top of the stack he kept chronologically arranged by the deck-chair in the corner of his hut.

On that Thursday evening his locking-up routine had progressed smoothly without hitch or hindrance. He had followed it to the letter; bolted the windows firmly and checked them rigorously to be sure they remained locked, then, with equal determination he snapped shut the ponderous iron padlock which secured the door and tested it three times, a significant number and the bare minimum he had allowed for when drawing up the matrix for this routine many years before. He took a few steps backwards and made a visual inspection of the walls and roof of the hut, or work establishment as he preferred to call it, then dipped his head ever so slightly in a nod of approval. Satisfied the hut was secure, he turned and was about to start for home when he stopped dead in his tracks. There was a man loitering by the rubbish bin just outside the gates.

Tramps were a common sight in those days although they were rarely seen so far from their usual haunts which was in the vicinity of the Municipal Park. Whenever he did come across one on his way to work or on a rare trip to the corner-shop for groceries, an involuntary shudder of horror would run through him. He was always surprised at their stark incongruity with the relatively clean and ordered environment into which they had strayed and took such flagrant advantage of. Their kind stank to high heaven of the rancid juices emanating from their own repugnant bodies and he had a good idea what they got up to with each other when drunk, and darkness hid them, and when most townspeople were conveniently, and thankfully, out of sight behind closed doors. They had a certain look about them, shifty, squalid, shameless and guilty; he could never get used to them, or accept them as relevant human beings, in fact he had realised some months previously that he actually despised them. Being filthy was bad enough but they were also corrupt, amoral and rotten to the core, choosing to live in utter chaos - drinking, pilfering and bickering - yelling and singing at such volume it was impossible to ignore them. Images of them drilled into his skull and laid eggs of hatred on his brain. Such was his indignation he had gone so far as to make several entries in his notebook expressing disbelief that the Authorities, by doing nothing, appeared to tolerate them. At least once, possibly as often as twice a year, but usually in summer when there seemed to be more of them about, he assured himself that one day he would put pen to paper and tell the Authorities these disgusting vagrants, these low-life heathens, were a disgrace to the uniforms they had once worn and demand, in no uncertain terms, that the streets be swept clean of them, then washed down thoroughly with bleach.

It's worth noting that his mother had lectured him at great length concerning the anti-sceptic properties of bleach.

His lips grew thin and curled into a snarl of disgust as he fixed his stare on the creature who so blithely threatened the order of his life. Allowing for the distance from which he was being observed, it seemed the tramp was short and stocky and dressed in some sort of dark evening suit. He could have been mistaken for a gentleman about town preparing to meet a lady for drinks before enjoying a fine dinner at a high class hotel, perhaps even the grandest of them all on the river front. The one with lawns sweeping down to the water's edge.

It was an involuntary movement but he cocked his head skywards and, ignoring the searing blueness and the swarm of wheeling swifts, he caught the merest snip of a sound, a strange melodic lilt drifting across the tarmacadam towards him, a warble so perfectly pitched, so unnaturally clear, it penetrated the thrum of traffic and burrowed deep into his ear. And there in the glowing silk of a summer's evening, his eyelids drooped and closed; with his face tilted to the sun he abandoned his senses to the sounds of the world he skimmed through every day and his expression took on the magical hue of sheer contentment. There, in that place, the car-park on the edge of the town centre, he remained perfectly still, leaning against the door jamb whilst in his mind the music swelled and soared to a crescendo of strings and tumbling brass - basso profondo - only to immediately crash with the sudden realisation he was also hearing the sound of someone singing. A man's voice, not a tenor, more a baritone. He shook his head and pretended to check the wooden walls for defects. He moved around the side of the hut nearest the road to gain better advantage and with his eyes hard closed listened fiercely. He was convinced. The tramp was the source of the singing - the scavenger at the gate, the vagabond who was rifling through the rubbish, his rubbish, helping himself, thieving! - and as he went about his business he sang at the top of his lungs, bobbing up and down, in and out of the bin, alternately muffled and throaty when reaching deep inside then the full force of a mighty crescendo when upright. He sang with gusto, with abandon, without an obvious care in the world.

The Car-park Attendant gritted his teeth and noted with a pang of contrition that the tramp was, to his surprise and in spite of everything, making a neat job of sorting his pickings on the pavement where, upon more determined scrutiny, he could just make out the white edges of a newspaper spread out flat like a table cloth.

He could hardly allow himself to become embroiled in a fracas by man-handling the tramp, roughing him up a bit - that would involve touching him, God forbid! - to claim his newspaper, to demand he hand it over. He could not risk drawing attention to himself. He dithered for a full ten minutes unsure how to resolve the puzzle, hoping the tramp would become bored or distracted and abandon his enterprise. But, far from it. The tramp emerged from the bin and gathered his treasure into a small mound rejecting only two items at the last minute, carefully replacing them in the bin, and folded the newspaper into a manageable package which he then placed carefully in a battered black leather briefcase. With a last look around to check he had left nothing of value behind and flicking dust from the shoulders of his jacket, the tramp kicked up his heels and set off at a brisk pace in the direction of the Municipal Park.

And so we arrive at the present day, Friday.

When he awoke, as on the previous mornings of the week, he knew there was an equal chance of him dying that day at an unspecified time in the afternoon. Regardless of that unhappy possibility such was his resolve to play by the rules, he continued to grind through his customary routines repressing any uninvited premonitions.

To us though, as all-knowing witnesses, the signs pointing to his impending demise are all too obvious. Let us review the evidence: to start with, getting himself ready for work had taken much longer than it should have done.

The matrix for his morning routine allowed only thirty minutes in total to wash, dress, eat breakfast and be out of the front door. Thirty minutes had always been ample time on every other morning, without exception, until that morning when he had been forced by certain events and unexplained happenings to seriously over-run: Firstly, shaving had not been conducted with the usual speed or precision because, if you remember, the light bulb in the bathroom had blown and the spare ones he bought yesterday remained on the counter at the hardware store: Secondly, for some inexplicable reason, while he slept his fingers had grown so engorged and bulbous they flapped around on the ends of his arms like angry, red, semi inflated balloons, it took enormous effort to operate them and even then they were so sore and clumsy it was as if they had become disconnected from the rest of him: Thirdly, without the usual sensitivity in his fingers he inadvertently pulled the knot of his Friday tie so tight he almost choked himself to death and took a full five minutes of painful tugging and fiddling to loosen and unravel it. Afterwards, he was so worn out he was forced to remain perched on the edge of the bed, gulping down great mouthfuls of air for a further two and a half minutes to recover from the strain. Fourthly, his shoelaces stubbornly refused to stay tied. His fingers were either too useless, tired or weak, but the knots of both shoes unravelled before he had even placed his feet on the floor. It took four attempts to secure them: Fifthly, just when he thought he was done, upon inspecting himself in the mirror he discovered a mark on his shirt collar which he attempted to sponge clean away, instead he only managed to make the stain much larger and more visible so he had to change his shirt. His scowling features darkened further at the realisation he was also forced to adjust his evening routine to include washing and ironing an extra shirt.

By the time he finished dressing and reached the bottom of the stairs he was red-faced and extremely agitated; his presence was as dark as a thunderous sky and his eyes flashed with fire. But the Torments were far from finished with him: the clock in the hall had mysteriously stopped; in a near-frenzy he checked his notebook to see when it was last wound up and found it should not have needed winding until tea time on Sunday. A ritual he never omitted.

It was, however, the penultimate item in the

morning's *catalogue of aggravations* that grieved him far more than any other, if for no other reason than it accentuated the malignant precariousness of human dependability. The milkman, despite a hitherto unblemished record of efficiency spanning many years, unpredictably failed to deliver the usual pint of milk to his doorstep forcing the Car-park Attendant to undertake the irksome task of mixing a jug of powdered milk just so he could make the tea for his flask.

We could dismiss all these occurrences, spiteful though they are, as trivial frustrations, but we know better than that by now. It would also be rational to assume if he, himself, possessed the aptitude for recognising psychic disorder then there would have been an equal chance he too could have seen the signs were beginning to look ominous and, perhaps, he might have put an end to his fateful game.

But he was late, irretrievably so according to his tried and tested schedule, and it was due to his lateness that the final straw came to be laid upon the unwitting camel's back, setting in motion a chain of events which was to ultimately seal his fate, or so we might believe.

He hurried at an ungainly trot as fast as his spindle

legs would carry him and with each step his breathing became increasingly laboured and stertorous. It was imperative he saw her, even a glimpse of her would do. It had lately become the single most important item in his daily routine. If he should fail, if she did not materialise without prompting or calling, if he did not catch sight of her in broad daylight, even through a window, it would unleash a chain of events which could easily end with him being killed - killing himself, more accurately - which is why, that morning of all mornings he should not have left so much to chance. He uttered a rare curse at his own stupidity but no sooner had he done so than his mother's voice oozed from the dark pregnant lobes of his brain into his mouth and ordered him to "Stop your whining and play the game, idiot boy!"

The sun slid behind a mountain of frothy white cloud.

He *must* see Poppy, it was essential. Her usual place was outside the hardware store heaving and stacking boxes, he pictured her red faced, standing back and fiddling with the buttons of her shop coat, head cocked to the side, considering the pavement display she had just created and which she proudly regarded as her very own territory.

"She *must* be there, she's *always* there!" he steamed under his breath hardly believing he had actually given voice to the words and he quickened the pace, his heart beating faster, one beat for every step. It was unthinkable that today of all days she should be hidden away, out of sight, at the back of the store doing something else. He could hardly contain the nervous bile engorging his throat and which was already beginning to form a solid mass in his chest.

He galloped faster and the tails of his coat brushed the grimy walls. He did not care. He pictured her face, flushed and anxious, she would surely miss him and wait. He pictured her shop coat straining with the weight of her breasts as she bent to pick up a box from the pavement; he was captivated by the sweetness of her round face, the fullness of her lips but his particular delight was the ring of scarlet flush which seemed always to appear around her neck whenever she caught him looking at her.

He was late, much later than usual but there was still a chance. Words hammered a rhythm in his head, "she will be there, she must be there, I will see her, I must see her." Everything would then be back to normal. "She must be there," what could be more important than making the shop attractive to customers? Of course she will be there. But no, he had missed his chance. He hovered at the crossing for as long as he dared risking being late to unlock the car-park, but in the end, at the very last minute, he had no choice but to go. There was no more time.

> *... Time! The one and only thing you*
> *need to make everything clean again.*
> *Deary me, what a shame ...*

Seconds ticked by and not for the first time did he experience the actual touch of time itself, those same seconds took shape and substance, swam in the blood which surged through his veins greasing his anxiety, hissing in his ears and with damning monotony beat nails into the back of his head. Realisation that she would not come hit him just as suddenly as a spear of sunlight drove to earth. He could wait no longer, she may never come and the game must be played out. He gripped the handle of his carrier bag until his knuckles were white. Nevertheless as two short minutes ticked by, he managed to bring his raging heart to heel and with its thunderous clamour no longer ringing in his ears, he crossed to the other side of the road the instant the lights changed.

It is germane to note at this juncture that not seeing her was the trigger for the most dangerous part of a special game he had concocted over the previous weekend and, crucially, was the reason he could be dead by the end of the day. He had played many such games in the past but he considered this to be the ultimate contest of pitting the unpredictable against the inevitable. It was to be his crowning glory and his swan song although the time had come to bring these games to an end because, you see, the excitement had gone out of them. He was sick and tired of winning all the games he had devised over the last three years, with every new game he had gradually raised the stakes until now, with his special game, his master-stroke, he was playing for his own life. With so much at stake, the preparations had been meticulous.

> ... *Mummy's so proud of her great big grown up boy*

Five days previously, on the Sunday evening, he had sat at the kitchen table, rivers of silver rain streaming down the blackened window panes, and lined up six pots of identically labelled crab paste and peeled off all the lids. Choosing one pot at random, he removed a flat teaspoon of the pungent concoction as accurately as he could measure then thoroughly mixed in an identical volume of arsenic powder. He carefully pushed the poisoned pot to one side and stirred, with a clean spoon, the meat in the other pots to match. It was essential they appeared identical. He replaced the lids, closed his eyes and moved the little pots around, scrambling them up to be doubly sure he could not identify the one with the poison. He placed them in a neat row on a shelf in the pantry, picked the first in line and proceeded to make sandwiches for Monday's lunch.

The game was elegant in its simplicity: if, as predicted, he saw Poppy on his way to work he would not eat his lunchtime sandwich but dump it in the bin at the car-park gates and he would know there was no possibility of poisoning himself that day. The inevitable sacrifice for cheating death was to go hungry until tea-time. If, on the other hand, he did not see her . . .

He died at twenty-seven minutes and sixteen seconds past four o'clock in the afternoon of one of the hottest days on record; discovered by a young woman wearing a pretty floral dress who worked during the week at a local hardware store and who, at the close of the day, returned to the care of the Sisters of the Sacred Heart at St. Hilda's Institution for Wayward Girls.

Part Four

The young woman who her gentleman (the Car-Park Attendant) referred to as *Poppy* for the sake of convenience, was untroubled by conventional intelligence. She was not stupid either, as some of the nuns at St. Hilda's believed her to be, she was merely slow to understand the nuances and complications of the modern world which, on many occasions resulted in her reacting to situations and predicaments naïvely or not reacting to them at all because she thought people would think her silly and laugh at her, which made her see red and go mad.

Her mind did not work in the way most people considered normal. For example, when she had a problem and the problem had an ending, with an outcome to which she needed to progress, in order to solve that problem, unless she thought about it one step at a time, in a straight line, and most importantly without interference from any of the other girls whose small white-painted rooms were on the same landing as hers, she would quickly become muddled. Words and faces, places and numbers would become jumbled. In an instant, the black dog would leap on her with one mighty bound and smother her, suffocate her - fear and anger rising within her - and with fists clenched and screaming like a banshee she would beat that black dog, beat it with venom dripping from her lips and brow, lightening darting from her eyes drilling fiery tunnels in the walls, incinerating those who would placate her. Worst of all, at some point in her fire-storm, her cervical muscles always relaxed and she inevitably felt the need to pee. This only served to increase her craziness as if it was not the demands of her own body but someone else imposing them upon her and her waters would flow where she stood. All this because she was simply not equipped to grasp the concept of time or place and their connections.

To comprehend the here and now, our brains rely on memories, learned behaviour if you will, fragments of the past, things done, consequences of tiny actions, the big things, smells and sounds, filed in such a way that they may be retrieved when needed. With this young woman it is entirely possible that the synapses responsible for the formation of memories somehow operated in isolation from the remainder of her mental capacities to the point that, although she was capable of recalling some of the specifics of an event such as names and colours (as well as the event itself), the deeper senses were locked away behind a spongy door through which they could only seep interminably slowly even though called upon to quickly step forward and be recognised. As such, in many respects, at least until the memories she had locked away had fully penetrated her consciousness, every remembrance of everything she had ever done was like a new dawn to her.

More often than not by the time she had worked out all the steps to solve the problem from beginning to end she had completely lost the thread of its context and the very reason for needing to solve the problem in the first place.

However there were exceptions.

It only registered with her that she had not seen her gentleman, her *Danny*, at all that morning when her boss heaved himself down the stairs from his apartment and loudly demanded a brew followed by, as always, an indulgent smack of his rubbery lips. While the kettle boiled on the gas ring, she stood in front of the clock and worked out the time by calculating how far the big and small hands were from pointing straight up. She fixed her eyes on twelve, *"That's the o'clock,"* she heard herself say and continued, counting on her fingers, *"two away from the o'clock is twelve, eleven, ten, so it's ten o'clock now, and I see him right at the beginning of the morning so that's ... um ... ages ago. Oh no!"*

She always saw him when she set up the displays and advertising boards on the pavement outside the store, it was her first and most important job of the day, the one she enjoyed the most, especially because she would get to see *Danny*.

How could she have missed him? How could it happen? A part of her believed that she had seen him but had stupidly forgotten and it was her mind playing tricks. She knew how stupid she could be. It was a cruel twist to the tumult already writhing in her belly.

From being a little girl she had learned the only way she could keep track of things was to cut the day up into small pieces which permitted her to pinpoint roughly where she was at any given time and what she should be doing. She saw *Danny* at the same time every morning, that was a very important piece, not seeing him, and worse not realising she had not seen him until much later, scared her. Something was wrong and she had to put it right. *"I must and I will"* she echoed Sister Bernadette, and the boss's tea remained stewing in the pot for as long as it took her to work out a plan.

It was an effort but steadily it dawned upon her that she did indeed have a plan. It had crept up on her without her realising it. The first thing was that she must ask the boss if it was all right to take the nice gentleman his light bulbs, at which request the boss pouted and rubbed his neck, "It's only round the corner," she said and her heart beat like a bird's wings when she saw the blubber of the boss's neck settle in a red doughnut around his collar which usually presaged a stern face and sometimes a wallop on the behind. "He, he works at the car-park," she blurted, "I'll only be 10 minutes, I'll be back in plenty of time for the bus, please sir boss, please sir." The second thing was that she needed to leave the store early and to show the boss there was still plenty of time for her to do all her jobs she counted off the hours on her fingers then repeated her plan over and over so she was sure he knew it too. At last, his big wet lips broke into a rubbery grin and he winked at her the same way he did when he told her a secret to be kept just between themselves.

Hours flew by and before she knew it, the time had come. The boss insisted on helping her off with her work coat and took the trouble to look her up and down to make sure she was neat and tidy. His gaze was steady when he told her how pretty she looked in her summer dress and pumps and kindly picked a hair from her cleavage before shooing her out the door with a chuckle and a playful smack on her behind which made her giggle - men do like their games!

It was only a short walk from the town centre to the car-park and in the sunshine she could not help but be happy, and when she was happy she liked to show it by smiling. She had never been alone with a man other than the boss but today she would see a man all by herself and she smiled a smile so wide her head could have broken in two.

She skipped along hugging herself, careful not to crush the light bulbs but swinging them back and forth anyway, joy bursting from every part of her. Soon she will be talking with him. *"He'll be my, he'll be my . . ."* she searched for the word, *"soul, something,"* she whispered, *"my soul, my soul, he will be my soul. Oh, what is it when people are the same, when they act the same way, when other people have done the same things to them and hurt them the same. Things I remember, he remembers because he's my soul . . ."*

She threw her arms wide and laughed out loud. She will actually talk to him properly no matter how hard it will be to make whole words, how long they take to come out, or even how stupid they sound. *"Soul-mate! He's my soul-mate,"* she suddenly whispered heavily, savouring the word. There will be things she must tell him, important things, and she knew in her heart, in her soul, that when she tells him he won't be nasty or laugh at her or shout at her for being slow and stupid. He'll understand. After all he's just like her so there will be no need for her to explain or say sorry.

At the entrance to the car-park she slowed to a stop and undid the top button of her dress. She had seen that in a movie once, a long time ago; a princess with shiny lips unbuttoned her blouse, and when the prince saw her, he lifted her onto his horse and gave her a big kiss, she wrapped her arms round him and they galloped over a hill to a little wooden house by a stream where they lived happily ever after. She was a princess now too floating through shimmering air across a steaming black river.

She drew closer and closer to his hut, his castle, the ground so hot beneath the soles of her thin shoes she was on tiptoe, dancing. She liked to dance, but she slapped her arms tight to her sides to resist temptation as she had been taught and became instantly sad and sought out her lips and cheeks with her fingertips to make sure she was still smiling. If only she could have seen it her face was ablaze and her eyes were glittering like stars, shining brightly as the flash-lights the Sisters used to wake the girls for midnight prayers.

They had taught her obedience, to serve their God without question and, most important of all, to keep feelings hidden, but today she did not care if people saw her joy or that she was dancing, she wasn't going to hide it. Of course, there will be gossip - she's not that stupid.

She arrived at *Danny's* hut - smaller than she imagined - and primped her hair, smoothed her dress which, in the stifling heat, was clinging tightly to her moist skin, and tapped on the window. There was no response so she pressed her nose against the glass and peered inside. She could neither see nor hear any movement, just black squares of glass staring dispassionately back at her. She consoled herself that he was sleeping or perhaps he had watched her coming and was hiding - icy fingers of humiliation began to grip her throat. She had to be sure so she moved to the farthest end of the window, cupped her palms around her eyes and strained to see through the blackness. Slowly her eyes became accustomed to the gloom and shadows began to drift away allowing familiar shapes to emerge. First, a foot with a shoe dangling from the heel then, as the murk retreated further into the corners, from the frayed edges of her vision a leg materialised, a leg with trousers rolled up to the calf revealing luminous white skin. She followed the leg along a seam of creased fabric up to a torso which was contorted at a peculiar angle to its limbs. Lastly a head was revealed to her, a grey mass nestling into the hooped cradle of a shirt collar its flesh quietly sagging like drips of wax from a candle.

It was a man's body lounging across a chair amongst a scattered chaos of nuts and bolts, hubcaps and tins. To her it seemed that someone had emptied a bag of rubbish all over the floor while her *Danny* slept.

There, in a car-park which had once been a field behind a picture house that had been flattened to make way for a shopping centre, uniformed young men with shiny faces squealed to a halt in a blaze of dust, in their glorious black cars, and began a frenzy of door slamming, clicking of stout heels, peering into the horizon, tutting their dry tongues and rifling through the pockets of jackets swinging from their shoulders for the paraphernalia of their job - pens, pencils and notebooks. To the young woman they appeared to be miraculous human beings, seeming to know precisely what they were doing and, incredibly, what they would be doing next.

Finding herself the centre of attention, she bit her knuckles and giggled, and in no time at all they had crowded around her and were firing questions which to her astonishment, when she answered, they listened to every word with bowed concentration. There was also much nodding and squinting sideways at one another while, with a lick of their stubby pencils, they transcribed everything she told them into little black notebooks. The ambulance windows had become a magnet for her swivelling eyes and when she caught her reflection the impression of herself was that of a dazzling beauty queen whose hair had become suddenly unruly though no match for her nimble fingers with which she swiftly prodded the strays back into place. She threw back her head and laughed at some unheard witticism and fiddled with the lobe of her ear followed by the clasp of a slim chain she wore around her glistening neck which bore a crucifix; Christ's feet nestled in the crease of her cleavage. She dragged her fingers across the moist skin, slowly and purposefully as if drugged, and firmly smoothed the bodice of her dress. She wafted muggy air with her slender hand to cool the expanse of her chest whilst gracing each of her courtiers with an uninhibited view of her beautiful face. She was amazed that they had come when she called, not that she had meant to call them, in fact she hadn't, she now remembered, someone else had.

It was all coming back to her, but the images were misty, the characters vaguely outlined and very still; she thought that perhaps it was all a big mistake because the gentleman - *did someone say he's dead?* - yes, in his hut -

oh, it's his office you know, it's got wooden walls and a sliding window - yes, we can see. Now miss, tell us everything you know - *Me? Everything? Gosh!* - start at the beginning please, and they all licked the lead of their pencils - *it must be a mistake because he only forgot his light bulbs . . . in the shop* - Which shop? - *Um, the hardware store on the corner of the High Street by the traffic lights with a zebra at the front . . .* She told them she had brought him the light bulbs in a brown paper bag, but when she got there he wouldn't answer when spoken to which she thought was quite rude but she didn't know he was dead at least not when she first saw him. *Is he really dead?* They all nodded. *Did he die because he forgot things and made a mistake by accident?* They quickly glanced at each other. *Poor man, poor gentle man.* No-one laughed.

She really wanted to help, to explain the circumstances in which she had found him but the instant she opened her mouth to speak faces in the crush swelled up before her and launched volley after volley of questions, one after another, from all sides - rat ta tat tat tat - and she gabbled, she knew it and couldn't help it: *Yes* - she liked working at the hardware store - *No* - her boss was always good to her - *For instance?* - he said he thought about her even when she wasn't there which, she said, was nice - *Yes* - she knew the dead man but he had never touched her, only smiled his funny little smile - *His name?* - Did she tell them she called him *Danny*? They all flicked back through the pages in their notebooks shaking their heads in unison.

She was made quite dizzy by the milling throng of musky young men dressed in matching shirt sleeves and ties, two of whom each wore a white coat and ducked in and out of the hut, all of them eager to demonstrate they were making a special effort just for her, treating her as somebody who had done something courageous rather than someone who had merely been lucky enough to discover a dead body.

They implored her to take all the time she needed and so she put on her thinking face; she made her forehead wrinkle and, as an extra touch, made her lips pucker up tight. They all tutted and muttered whilst stabbing their tongues with their pencils to moisten the tip. To the best of her ability, with her facial contortions, she showed them she was thinking really hard about what they called the sequence of events and which they had asked her to recall.

However, regardless of her unshakable concentration, before she could think of even the first thing to say, an image of Sister Boniface rose up before her, stern and brittle, and with a voice like a crystal bell she began issuing instructions, "Listen child, everything has it's place! One thing always follows another, always! Never let it be said if I told you once or a million times, observe the *sequence of consequences* and your feet will always point onwards up the path of righteousness. If you don't and they do, your feet that is, you'll end up doing the Devil's work for him!" Sister Boniface had frequently lamented the selfless sacrifice she was forced to endure for the sins of the girls in her charge but she felt herself to be all the more replete because of it which, of course, was a source of great relief to the girls.

The young woman allowed Sister Boniface to remain in her head while she curled the tip of her moist pink tongue over the ruby gloss of her upper lip in yet another wanton display of unrestrained concentration and, as one, the crowd of courteous young men heaved towards her so close she fancied she could feel the heat of their breath. She closed her eyes but then after only a moment or two her mouth and lips ceased working and became still, her brow cleared and her chest resumed its quiet rhythm. She slowly shook her head several times to dislodge one last stubborn doubt and began her version of events by telling them she was certain someone else had been there too, but the other person had only been there after she had seen the dead gentleman through the window. It was probably a customer of the car-park because he had a car but she hadn't seen where he came from and could not remember what he looked like. She clearly remembered it was he who broke the door of the hut and went in to see if *Danny* was alright and then she remembered in a sudden rush that the nice *customer gentleman* made her sit on the running board of his car while he ran to the telephone box across the road to call for help. It was only a matter of minutes after he came back that they heard the wail of sirens rushing toward them. In her mind's eye she could see the customer's face close to hers, checking her over to make sure she was fine and because they were on the same team, he said, and because they had saved the day he had kissed her and patted the hand in her lap as if it was a pet. *No* - she did not know when or to where he had disappeared.

When nervous she licked her lips, something she had observed people doing when they were concentrating on important things, at least that is how it appeared to her. She had also noticed that some people, when they licked their lips, instead of tucking their tongue away afterwards, left it in the corner of the mouth sticking out as if ready for action, ready to do something, which is where she left hers until called upon to answer more questions. She was beginning to feel irritated, cornered.

No - she hadn't seen if the dead man's tongue was sticking out, but now she had time to think about it she fancied it was but she couldn't be certain because it was dark in the shed. "Was it pitch black?" asked an especially grave young man with wavy hair and blond eyebrows. *Pitch black? Um, yes I think so.* She liked the sound of pitch black. "If it was that dark in there how could you see him?" *No, not pitch black, prob'ly more like grey black* - she explained there was a tiny little hole in the shed's wall below the sliding window and that she had looked through it and had seen his face and hands, but not his whole head because it was too small - not his head, the hole, the hole was too small - and he was turned away from her in any case. Frowning, the young man scribbled her answer in his notebook and her tummy lurched, she longed for it not to be over. She was afraid she had disappointed them and wished with all her heart for more time to make them understand.

She quickly told them that she saw him, the dead man, every day in the morning - *boss sets his watch by him* - she said he is nice, was nice, the gentleman not the boss; no, the boss is nice too but the gentleman is, was, you know extra nice - "Yes, yes we get it!" piped up a barefaced youth who looked far younger and more stupid than any of the others. She faltered but nothing could distract her for long; they had never spoken to each other, she said, and she didn't know his name but called him *Danny* anyway because he looked like a Danny and the name fitted snug as a bug. The policemen seemed pleased with her again and smiled at each other, all except the stupid one who, she noticed, had a flimsy moustache like a half drowned spider, all wet. He asked her for the second time, in a horrible squeaky voice if she had ever been to his house and if he had, you know, touched her. She gave him one of her looks, so hard her eyeballs shivered, and he sniggered, spluttering spittle from thin blue lips which he wiped with a large bright red handkerchief, then patted his brow. She saw he was sweating like a pig and decided to ignore him. Turning her shoulder against him and gathering the rest of them to her, leaning inwards like a conspirator, in a hoarse whisper, she told the others huddled all around her that she hadn't seen *Danny* that morning, she didn't know why and it was a shame because he could have collected the light bulbs himself, the ones he accidentally left in the store the day before, then she wouldn't have needed to bring them to him and she wouldn't have found him and he *prob'ly* wouldn't be dead at least no-one would have found him dead, not for ages. She abruptly stopped speaking and fell silent.

After a minute or two the brave young men smiled at her and nodded. "And that, as they say, is that," announced the singularly unsmiling stupid one and they all shuffled their feet whilst making slippery eyes at each other, half grimacing. Taking her downcast silence as a cue, one by one they each stuck a pencil stub behind their ear and shuffled away. She held out her arms palms upwards and implored the fast disappearing crowd - *can anyone tell me if people are still alive even when you can't see them?* Afterwards, when reflecting on the day, she was not sure if she had asked the question aloud although she did finally recall that no-one had taken the trouble to answer her.

And that was the end of her story. There was nothing more she had to say.

One hour later and the excitement has evaporated; the policemen have put on their jackets and driven off; the ambulance driver has taken his jacket off and carted the Car-park Attendant's body away. The principal actors have departed the stage and all that remains are sundry props which lie where they fell. The earth has finally unglued from the furnace heat of the day and a sluggish stream of cooler air drifts down the avenues which radiate like the spokes of a wheel from the car-park at its hub. A sultry peace has descended upon a world which to all outward appearances remains unchanged.

A nonchalant young mother with thrusting arms pushes a pram at speed along the boulevard heading for home, leaving behind her the inebriating delights of the town. In her wake follows the reassuring baritone drone of insects and the soprano chatter of birdsong. Beneath the trees she too flits between light and shadow.

Some way into the distance wandering towards us comes a teenage girl, her clothes emblazoned with the names of important fashion houses, her make-up is flawless though her face glistens uncomfortably with a waxy sheen. Her hair swings loose and tumbles the full length of her back. It springs up and down in relaxed coils, constantly in motion, glowing in the remaining sunlight. She wears an expression of absolute boredom. Her eyes, dead; her spirit flattened, crushed, and the act of breathing too wearisome to endure. Attached to her hand is a small child dressed in sailor shorts and tunic. He drags his fingertips along a tide line of sooty grey road-dirt thrown up by passing vehicles against trees, railings and a bus stop where he is finally and abruptly tugged to a halt. There they stand hand in hand, side by side, waiting, their eyes fixed on a distant point somewhere along the road.

Behind them is a quaintly decorated cottage. From the first floor window a house-proud woman vigorously shakes a shaggy rug and the dust tumbles in lazy drifts onto the leaves and flowers of her small, beautifully tended garden. And there on the corner beneath the wall which surrounds that garden stand a man and a woman. Secret lovers, they touch and engage each other's gaze a few seconds too long, their lips parted just so, both abandoning their souls to earthly pleasures, both compose their facial features to exhibit unbridled desires, for surely theirs is the purest living light shining in a drab, colourless world. They briefly pull apart only to crush together once more, locking themselves in an eternal embrace so overwhelmed by the heat of their own passion they barely manage to remain upright. It must be obvious to anyone that they would rather die than be parted. In truth, they inhabit an alternative existence where every child exists to be smiled at, gazed upon with such longing it seems their lives would be rendered worthless, their desires so utterly pointless, if they were never to possess for themselves such a blesséd child. In their Utopia the lion quite possibly does lie down with the lamb, a mother more than likely could never die of a broken heart and a human spirit would never, ever, be allowed to starve for want of warmth and compassion. In the present, their existence is as divorced as the span between the sun and moon from the reality of being a husband and a wife, of having children and a family home somewhere else with someone else.

We are now almost at the entrance to the car-park and making his way towards us comes an office worker sporting a regulation haircut, his jacket draped carelessly over one stooped shoulder and carrying a black leather briefcase with buckle straps looped over the front flap typical of the kind used by middle ranking civil servants. His eyes a-glitter at the extravagance of having time on his hands to do whatever he pleases, a comfortable smile broadens over his face as he walks along with a wide legged, easy swagger. We have learned much from the events of the day, the principal lesson being, mundane as it might seem, that something inescapably certain can be suddenly overturned by something equally uncertain and unpredictable. As such we might be forgiven a derisory chuckle at this Jack-the-Lad about town, so carefree, celebrating his temporary freedom from the daily grind. Of course he can have no idea he has played such a significant role in the demise of our Car-park Attendant. How could he? At the gates, he drops the newspaper he has been carrying under his arm into the bin then suddenly breaks his stride to cross over the road, putting a safe distance between himself and a dishevelled old man wearing a frayed raincoat tied up with string.

The tramp, who hums a tune under his breath, makes straight for the rubbish bin and dives inside. He pulls out the young man's newspaper and places it neatly at his feet. Next he extracts a half eaten apple which he holds up in triumph and sings, "Tah dah!" and begins to polish what remains of its skin on the remnants of his sleeve. He is just about to take a huge bite when he espies the car-park hut and peers furtively around. Something in his water tells him something is not right. He espies the back of a young man disappearing round the corner and there, some way off into the distance, is a woman preoccupied with her bra strap, pushing a pram with her one free hand; in the foreground, a girl and a child stand at a bus stop. Apart from these incidental characters the coast is clear and there is nothing that poses an immediate threat so he turns to look at the hut once more. Nothing moves or stirs to warn him and his gnarled face begins to close up on itself like a woodlouse that curls into a ball for protection, his chin bends upwards and touches the tip of his pitted nose while his beetling black brows fold downwards almost covering the dusty round mounds of his cheeks.

He ambles over to the hut, humming and mumbling nonsense, swatting flies real and imagined. Through the window he can see a dim light burning from a single bulb that hangs by a wire from the ceiling. There is no-one inside. Curiosity draws him in and he creeps through the door and when his eyesight has grown accustomed to the gloom he stands in bewildered excitement among mountains of treasure.

His eyes, the colour of smoked fish, long used to lurking in the shadowy recesses of their sockets, peel back their lids and stand out on stalks. He wraps his arms around himself and grinning like a lunatic ogles silver dishes, jewel encrusted goblets and bottles of the finest crystal scattered all over the floor among what look to him like nuggets of purest gold. He whoops and smacks his thigh. In his excitement the muscles of his neck and throat have become so thick he can hardly breathe, not that he cares because from the moment he stepped into that place he knew the course of his life had been changed forever.

He simply cannot believe his good fortune and continues to beat his leg until completely overcome with exhaustion and plonks himself down into a rickety old chair where he sits breathing hard, his face alight with a beaming smile, awestruck by the gifts bestowed upon him and all the while his bony fingers tap upon the smooth surface of a stack of newspapers at his side.

What more could he wish for? He has both comfort and shelter as well as the promise of an uninterrupted night's sleep but can it be the Fates have read his mind and know the true extent of his desires. His rapture is complete when he discovers a feast, on a little shelf by his elbow is a plastic lunch-box containing a crab paste sandwich. As it happens he has found one of the same sandwiches in the bin by the car-park gate every day for the past few days. He has grown to rather like them.

As he peels off the plastic lid he blesses his good fortune and licks his lips in anticipation.

The end

Swell

Thank you very much for reading my book, I truly appreciate the time and attention you have given me. If you enjoyed it, may I ask you to take a moment and leave a review at your favourite retailer.

Ever yours,

Rivenrod

Brief history of the author:

Born in Berkshire, United Kingdom | School in Dorset & Berkshire | College in Somerset | University in London | Explored Europe, North Africa, Malaysia, South America | Worked in Advertising | Grew children | Moved & shook in global corporations | Escaped the lunacy | Artist & Writer |

If you would like to know more go to www.rivenrod.com

Connect with me: Weblog: www.rivenrod.com | Twitter: @Rivenrod | eMail: rivenrod@rocketmail.com

My paintings, drawings and prints:
www.seat214.com/artists/rivenrod

Forthcoming titles by Rivenrod:

Miscreation (Expected publication: February/March 2016)

Miscreation plots the growth of a boy from childhood into adulthood in a series of deceptively light inter-connected stories marking the stages of his life. His early background is privileged and mundane - his frustrations are recognisable as those of a child, his observations of life going on around him are cynical and ever so slightly twisted. As he evolves, he develops his own brand of humanity which not only reveals him as someone ill equipped for the adult world but also as a miscreant. His spirit (pneuma) is unnaturally linked with bestial flesh (soma) by way of his corrupt soul (psyche). There are a great many questions left hanging in the air but the main one, as always, is whether he finds a way to suppress his demons or allows them to exist unrestrained.

Finally, he becomes his own creation with truly shocking and totally unexpected consequences.

Excerpt from Miscreation: Chapter *one - Pain: Five years old*

The boy's early childhood was not unusual.

He was born without much fuss in a village hospital in Berkshire and for several months his full-time occupation was to process milk and then mashed food into an almost constant stream of industrial strength mortar which he shot from both ends without prejudice or favouritism in a single shade of puke yellow.

Ever the follower of expediency even at such a young age, he did not bother to learn to crawl but progressed directly to waddling. He also bypassed the walking stage. While his peers tottered like blindfolded tightrope walkers doddering from one piece of furniture to another, he quickly developed a kind of headlong gallop; an arms back, head down, uncontrolled, full tilt, run which was all very well but the family home was a triumph of modern open plan living with numerous glass doors, windows at floor level, open stair treads and absolutely no stair rail to spoil the sweep of the architect's vision (who also happened to be his father). Inevitably he had to be rescued on several occasions after falling feet first through the stairs. Inconveniently, his parents neglected to provide crash mats in the danger zones, an oversight which led to the boy sporting bumps and bruises almost continuously throughout his toddler-hood.

Eventually, like almost every other child, he learned to talk and to read and within an unusually short period of time had progressed sufficiently to be able to hold rudimentary conversations with anyone and everyone, anywhere and everywhere, mostly about varieties of food, the availability of those foods and whether it would be too much trouble to have some of the aforementioned food immediately.

Even in infancy, when his peers were struggling to make sense of those large brightly coloured letter blocks, words on a printed page held few mysteries. Numbers on the other hand were a different matter entirely. The purpose of mucking about with numbers eluded him and he grew to fear them as harbingers of misfortune, with some justification. It seemed to him that something bad always happened to him after either one of his parents counted to three.

"Perhaps that's only as far as they can count," he

thought hugging himself for being clever enough to count to seven.

It seemed to him, numbers were too rigid, too unbending and extremely bad tempered. There was only ever one way to interpret them and the maverick spirit within his eager young breast could not get to grips with their anal discipline. Overall, though, it would be fair to say most areas of learning did not pose much difficulty for him. Even numbers would one day reveal their secrets in the face of his somewhat obsessive persistence. He possessed a quick and flexible mind even if he was inclined to perilous flights of fancy from time to time. No, not "flights of fancy" as in a manner of speaking but actual real life *flights*, of fancy.

So it was that growing up, whilst a number of academic subjects as well as lessons in life and some experiences caused him fleeting pain or discomfort, he first learned about real pain when he was five years old. It was to be an event he would recall with absolute clarity for the rest of his life. It was a hard lesson, cruel too and what is more, it was not inflicted upon him by anyone else and had nothing whatsoever to do with numbers but everything to do with mischief of his own making.

Oh My God! (Expected publication: August/September 2016)

Despite his physical drawbacks Prom, our leading man, does indeed recognise the world he inhabits however, he gradually comes to realise not everything is as he ought to remember it. It's the little things he notices first like the unnatural way rain crawls down a window pane. And then there are some more significant predicaments like the sex-mad girlfriend he never knew he had.

    He is guided through this increasingly alien world by Scissorsnip an unusual character who describes himself as a Guardian Angel but the jury's out on that one. Make your own mind up.   The tale is ably supported by a rich cast of bit players in lavish settings all described with acute attention to every conceivable detail. The culmination of the story will leave your imagination reeling and, when all is finally revealed, will make you wonder how you could have missed so many important clues to the reality of the situation.

Excerpt from Oh My God!: *Part one - Space and Existence*

"Oh my God, I am soooooooo ahead of my time!"

I was expecting the intrusion. Since he first erupted into my life a week ago, it has become his habit to descend upon me at four o'clock in the afternoon every day, and here he is, unfortunately as reliably punctual as ever. I have no recollection what it was that first motivated me to blindly follow his instructions regarding the preparations I must make for his arrival, I do know however that every day at precisely 3:58pm I find myself stopping whatever it is I am doing: I reconnect my fountain pen with its cap and lay it to rest vertically beside the column of manuscript I have presumably been working on and then, to the best of my limited ability, I return the scattered jumble of reference books to their proper places. Whilst doing so, without fail and on pain of bringing down something nasty but as yet unspecified upon my head, as instructed I must insert a length of red ribbon between each of the pages I have been referring to during the day ensuring that the tail is at least long enough for him, the

Tyrant, to comfortably reach from the sprawling comfort of his fire-side chair. Having accomplished all that, I am then to face the door through which he will make his entrance, "The front of one's head is so much more, er, relevant don't you think," he had said, "so many more lines to read and inwardly digest although some faces, a great many actually, a *very* great many on reflection, make me sick to the stomach. Nevertheless I insist you face me and face me you shall!"

Today however I rebel. I have not placed the red ribbons and at the exact moment of the appointed hour I did my level best to remain staring out of the window, with my back to the door, when it flew open. Pointless really because the instant I heard his hand grip the door knob and in the fraction of a second it took me to blink, I was just as suddenly and completely involuntarily turned to face him. *Dynamics!* was the word that lingered like an echo in a dark and dank smugglers cave.

Today he wears wine; a smoking jacket the colour of burgundy draped over narrow shoulders which rise to a point level with his ears. His legs, thin, are encased in muscadore brushed velvet, and his torso in a rosé pink shirt with buttons of garnet set in old gold fashioned into the everyday objects - a wellington boot, a coffin and a padlock amongst others. The ensemble is finished off by two bow ties, one, pale green (Vinho Verde no doubt) was worn straight and slightly tighter about the neck than the other which was a fiery ruby red set at a careless angle, as if arrested mid spin and applied to the portrait as an afterthought rather than an important statement of fashion which observation the present occupant would almost certainly prefer.

His whole being exudes spikiness, sharpness; his manner, his frame, his physique bears no soft edges whatsoever and of all his angular features, his face is the most startling.

Framed by the wings of a stiffly starched collar, it is a crescent moon with smoke blackened craters in the depths of which his eyeballs roll first one way then the other in continuous motion. His lips are small and thin, slivers of liver which neither part nor purse, not even when sipping tea, but ripple along their length with the lazy slowness of a river punt's bow wave. His nose, on the other hand is an extravagance. Straight from the forehead, crooked midpoint at thirty-three degrees with dark cavernous nostrils that surely contain secrets of their own and finally as an additional layer of gruesomeness, the skin of his cheeks has been tugged so very tightly in order to cover the full extent of his massive cheekbones, most viciously it seems judging by the appearance of tiny ruptures around his eyes. So tight in fact that the skin in places is transparent. The entire effect is hideous in the extreme and in my opinion, in so far as it counts for anything, if he was being truthful about his ability to appear only to a few *carefully selected* people, it is fortunate so few will ever have the misfortune to catch sight of his face.

He coughed quietly as a reminder he was still waiting.

Despite my best efforts to appear nonchalant, I am afraid my irritation must have been written large on my face because he shot me a bolt of acid then pulled his cheeks into a grotesque impersonation of a smiling ghoul causing the skin to rip a little further at the temples. I began to choke behind my hand but recovered sufficiently to tentatively venture, "How so, ahead of your time?"

From time to time further details of other publications will be posted on www.rivenrod.com

Made in the USA
Charleston, SC
19 August 2015